WILD AND
UNCANNY TALES

Marc Harris

First published 2023
by Rowanvale Books Ltd
The Gate
Keppoch Street
Roath
Cardiff
CF24 3JW
www.rowanvalebooks.com

A CIP catalogue record for this book is available from the British Library.
ISBN: 978-1-914422-37-9
Hardback ISBN: 978-1-914422-38-6
eBook ISBN: 978-1-914422-36-2

TABLE OF CONTENTS

INTRODUCTION

I have always had a deep fascination with both the natural and supernatural worlds, and, in particular, Gothic ghost stories. Within these pages, you will encounter that fascination and discover tales that entertain, undoubtedly scare, and maybe even make you laugh.

I have been inspired, for many years now, by the writings of Bram Stoker and Sheridan le Fanu, whose book *Carmilla*, was the inspiration for Stoker's *Dracula* itself. One of my favourite books and films is the wonderful *The Woman in Black*. Both the book, and the film, will chill you to your bones.

My fascination with nature, and haunting atmospheres, is also a prominent feature within my stories, and in combining my two passions, I hope you discover something that interests you and keeps you reading until the end of my book. I have included a few poems which I feel complement the short stories. Primarily, I hope you enjoy this book and, after reading, come away with a sense of what might, or might not, be out there – I will let you decide.

Sweet dreams.

KEEPING SECRETS

The great house, dark and brooding with its high granite walls, dominated the grounds. Its austere presence had been part of a wider, spartan landscape of peat bogs, heather, and gorse for generations. It had survived all that nature could throw at it – the howling winds and fierce gales, and the freezing winters, which had fractured and pitted all that surrounded it.

Within the landscape, the hiker moved with speed and purpose, following the coastal path which threaded its way along the clifftops before descending a steep incline through the sand dunes and onto the beach. The sweeping sands were soon swallowed up by an icy, cloying mist which drifted shoreward – almost without perception, from far out to sea. He trained his camera on the horizon, but little moved apart from the swirling mists and the winds carrying them.

Animals had left their marks in the dunes. There were rabbit droppings everywhere, along with the tracks of badgers, foxes, and a myriad variety of birds. Marram grass, thistles, and the stunted shapes of gorse bushes sank their roots into the sand, eking out an existence – forever blown and battered by the seasonal storms which had their origins far out in the Atlantic Ocean.

As dusk approached, the hiker retraced his steps, leaving the beach and following the coastal path inland until he came to the sanctuary of the bothy.

He showered, changed his clothes, lit a blazing fire in the hearth, then sat in the armchair dozing until he drifted into a deep sleep.

Outside, as night fell, the diurnal creatures, too, sought the sanctuary of their nests and beds. In the pale moonlight, the nocturnal creatures came alive and went about their business as the night progressed and the silver stars twinkled in the sky.

At daybreak, the young man hiked to the great lake, then settled into the hide where he hoped to observe, then photograph, anything of note. He stared into the mists, which appeared to rise from the lake's very surface itself. In the distance, a raven cried, and to his right, a pair of secretive water rails called hauntingly from the cover of the reed beds. Beyond the far edge of the lake, the great house, empty now for some fifty years, loomed large in the distance.

He held his powerful binoculars to his eyes, then began to scan the water and beyond.

He remained in the hide as the day progressed. He watched as huge carp rose from the lake depths to suck on water snails which clung to weeds in the lake margins, where tangles of broken branches and tree roots gave sanctuary to the fry of many fish. Mallard, coot, swans, and a pair of great-crested grebe cruised the water's surface, but as the clock ticked towards late afternoon and the mists dissipated and the sun began to sink below the horizon, the young man was yet to spot any of the more unique things he had come to photograph.

At dusk, as the temperature dropped, his breath began to steam and he began to shiver. He put on his woollen hat and thick fleece, then wrapped a scarf tightly around his neck.

In the grounds, and in the great house itself, strange things began to stir.

The first to appear was the boy's face at the window. The young man pointed the camera's long lens in the direction of that window, pressed a button, and the shutter clicked.

Beside the lichen-encrusted fountain, which had ceased functioning many years before, the pale, almost ethereal figures of two young girls attired in long, flowing silk dresses appeared as if from nowhere and began to dance – moving with such grace, purpose, and poise as they circled the fountain.

The faint sound of giggling drifted across the expanse of water and into the hide.

The young man pointed the lens in the girls' direction, pressed a button, and the camera clicked once again.

It was not long before the adults began to appear.

In one of the shattered glasshouses, the wizened, stooped figure of an elderly gardener and his assistant tended to the soil. And across the neatly trimmed lawns bounded a big black dog, chasing a ball thrown by its master and mistress who were dressed in the finest of Edwardian evening attire.

In the hide, the young man continued to take photographs, until a bell tolled in the tiny family chapel in the shadow of the great house, and once again the mists rose from the lake's surface, enveloping all, including the hide, in a clammy white shroud which remained until first light.

In the grounds, and in the great house, nothing now moved, and the spectral figures had simply vanished. All was silent and at peace.

At daybreak, the young man made the long trek back in the direction of the sanctuary of the bothy.

And the photographs he had taken, of the boy's face at the window, the dancing girls, the wizened gardener and his assistant, the master and mistress, and the big black dog which bounded across the lawns of the great house chasing a ball...

Well, what do you think?

Of course, no image, of human or dog alike, was actually captured, or for that matter, would ever be captured.

And, perhaps, in his heart of hearts, the young man had always known this.

The great house would always keep its secrets.

He sighed and shrugged his shoulders, threw another log onto the blazing fire, then settled into his armchair and dozed into a deep, dream-filled sleep.

Outside, when darkness fell, a cold, cloying mist drifted shoreward, almost imperceptibly, from far out in the Atlantic Ocean. And in the grounds of the great house, and in the great house itself, the first of the strange things began to stir.

THE LEGEND OF ESME BELL

The great fog bank swept across the sea, rolling in from far out in the Atlantic Ocean, creeping across jagged rocks, the beach, and up the precipitous cliffs to envelop the tiny church in a pale and clammy shroud, a sinuous, billowing cloak which penetrated the heart and very soul of the ancient structure.

In the distance, a foghorn boomed. On top of the church tower, the flag of Saint Piran fluttered like a rag doll in the wind. The wind grew fiercer, pounding and battering the little church, and whistling amongst the gravestones, until, finally, the great sea-fog lifted, melting into the ether.

In the bell tower, the diminutive bell began to toll incessantly, until even its soundings were snuffed out by the howling wind and sheeting rain.

And it was on such a night, some two hundred years ago, that the *Mermaid* – a one-hundred-foot wooden-hulled schooner bound for America carrying a cargo of timber, whisky, rum, and twenty poor souls, was lost, lured to her doom in that most unforgiving and fiercest of Atlantic storms by the lanterns of wreckers. Wreckers whose only interest was the profit to be made by the looting of the ship's precious cargo.

Legend has it that on the anniversary of the wrecking of the *Mermaid*, if a fierce storm is raging, the waif-like figure of a young girl can be seen, moving about the rugged cliffs and battered beaches. A pale figure wrapped in a cloak of seaweed, with flowing blonde locks and a haunted look in her eyes. A lost soul who carries an oil lamp, which she swings back and forth, signalling frantically towards the sea.

It is said that the girl's spirit will not rest until she hears the sound of her mother's voice, carried from deep in the ocean, on the tides and currents and those fierce Atlantic winds.

And only when the storm abates, and dawn breaks, and she has heard that soothing voice, will the soul of Esme Bell settle amongst the headstones of the church on that rugged clifftop. A church where she was laid to rest some two centuries ago, alongside her father and younger brother.

Today, on the rugged coast of Cornwall, the early autumn sun is shining, and there is barely a breeze to trouble the flag of Saint Piran. The perfume of wildflowers and the melodious sound of birdsong adorn the graveyard; the diminutive bell is silent – and nineteen of the poor souls who perished with the *Mermaid* sleep peacefully in hallowed ground.

CONGER

Man's-waist thick,
fathomed at depth –
wrecking jaws,
wrecking flesh.

Spawned in black,
greased against the sea,
hooked, trawled –
gaffed, clubbed,
and clubbed again on the neck.

Then pictured on paper,
malevolent in death –
longer than a man's body.

THE MISTRESS OF THE WRECK

The great eel swam sinuously through the shattered wreck of the warship. She was over twenty years old, having been born a year before the sinking of the corvette, which had been split in two by a mine during the war before settling on its starboard side on the seabed.

Fishermen knew the giant eel well, for she had been hooked and lost on many occasions.

The great eel could swim backwards too, and now, as she snaked tail-first inside the rusting, barnacle-encrusted funnel which had become her lair, she could sense a change in the currents which swirled around the wreck.

A powerful storm was brewing, and it was time for even one as muscular as her to seek sanctuary.

The crew of the *Snake-Hunter* were wise to remain in port and wait out the storm, which, even inside the breakwater, whipped white horses against her hull. Beyond the breakwater, the Atlantic Ocean raged in the darkness.

Lying in his bunk, skipper Dave Barrett tossed and turned as the rain hammered like nails against the deck above his head. Smiler, a veteran of many legendary conger trips, lit a cigarette and watched the blue smoke drift towards the ceiling. A faint orange glow emanated from the single lightbulb, which flickered intermittently, casting dark, eerie shadows about the cabin.

With the storm forecast to last until first light, the fishermen waited with nervous anticipation for the winds to subside.

Some four hours later, with the sea much calmer and only a slight swell, the forty-foot trawler was steaming south-east in the direction of the battle-scarred fishing grounds.

With the baits cast, the fishing boat drifted silently over the wreck.

Hundreds of feet below, the mackerel flappers and whole pouting bait dangled enticingly only feet above the lair of the great eel.

Shoals of smaller fish drifted in and out of the sanctuary of the wreck. Cod, pollack, and haddock – creatures which the giant eel preyed upon – meandered about the rusting, coral-encrusted structure of the ship. Brittle stars, spider crabs, and one of the corvette's resident lobsters, moved at their own inimitable pace across the debris field which stretched for a quarter-of-a-mile over the seabed.

On the deck of the *Snake-Hunter*, Dave Barrett and Smiler waited for that first familiar tug on their lines.

With the coming of dusk, they knew their chances of catching a big eel increased dramatically.

As darkness fell, the slight swell which had buffeted the trawler's hull for most of the afternoon diminished, and the *Snake-Hunter* became becalmed in a glassy sea which stretched to the horizon. Ten miles east of the fishing boat, the beam of Scare-Point lighthouse flickered in the soft, pale moonlight.

A small ray was the first fish to be pulled from the depths, followed by a diminutive codling and a pollack weighing five pounds. Each fish was quickly dispatched by a sharp blow to the head from a heavy priest.

At that moment, the eerie calm which had engulfed the fishing boat was suddenly exacerbated when a freezing mist rolled in from far out in the Atlantic, enveloping the crew in a shroud as white as snow.

Hundreds of feet below, in the inky blackness of her lair, the Mistress of the Wreck, the huge conger, had sensed the bait.

The great eel stirred, then loosened the grip of her tail on the twisted metal inside the corvette's hull.

She swam out into open water, cautiously circling the bait, first from below and then from above, nuzzling it with her sensitive yet cavernous mouth.

The powerful currents made the bait unstable, forcing it both upwards and sideways in a sudden, violent movement. And the great eel, overcome by instinct, clamped her massive jaws around the vicious steel hook. It bit deep into her flesh.

On board the *Snake-Hunter*, Dave Barrett watched the powerful rod bend in half. Line zipped from his reel as the great eel turned and twisted, thrashing her massive head back and forth in an attempt to free herself from the cruel hook which had torn the inside of her mouth.

Instinctively, Smiler grabbed his skipper from behind, clinging to him like a limpet, desperate to prevent him from being dragged overboard.

Hundreds of feet below, in the icy depths of the Atlantic Ocean, the great eel was already backing into the barnacle-encrusted funnel.

But the tackle on board the forty-foot trawler was strong. In fact, it was the strongest and most robust fishing tackle Barrett had ever brought to these fishing grounds.

Whatever the cost, he wanted that fish on board his vessel, and he would stop at nothing until he had claimed his prize.

Deep in the dark waters, the eel's body was now entirely inside the funnel. But the violence of her struggles had only forced the vicious hook deeper into her mouth. There was no way she could dislodge it, and severing the wire trace to which it was attached was proving impossible.

Slowly, imperceptibly, the skipper of the *Snake-Hunter* began to gain ground on the giant fish. Inch by inch, she was pulled from the funnel, then dragged across the pitted, rocky ground of the debris field, before being yanked without ceremony towards the surface of the ocean.

In desperation, the great eel continued to thrash and twist in a futile attempt to break the fishing line. The line held firm. And now, she was being dragged ever closer to the surface, where Smiler, who still had hold of his skipper in a tight embrace, waited with exhausted anticipation to impale her with his needle-sharp gaff.

After a fight lasting more than two hours, the giant eel's head broke the ocean's surface for the very first time in her life. She twisted her body in one final, violent movement before flopping limply in what was now simply a gentle swell.

With sweat pouring from his brow in torrents, Dave Barrett reeled in his line with what strength he had left, bringing the great eel closer to his boat. Smiler, who had by now released his grip on the skipper, stood next to him, panting like a dog, gaff in hand.

Momentarily, their jaws dropping, both men stared in utter disbelief at the sheer size of their exhausted quarry.

Then, when the stricken eel was no more than a foot from the boat, the eerie grip of the swirling mists seemed to intensify.

Wisps of a new kind of mist appeared as if from nowhere, some rising from the very depths themselves, from a place so dark that it was incomprehensible to the crew of the *Snake-Hunter*.

Barrett and Smiler could only look on in abject horror as those mists began to form into the shape of a human arm, and then a human hand: a vaporous, skeletal hand, with fingers and a thumb, whiter than the whitest of snow.

As the bony fingers of the hand reached forwards to cut the wire trace which held the great eel, Smiler toppled backwards onto the wooden deck, hitting his head and knocking himself unconscious. The sharpened point of the gaff landed only inches from his throat.

In a whirlpool of water, the giant eel was sucked into the depths.

Sometime later, in his cabin below deck, Smiler sat shivering and babbling uncontrollably, an icepack pressed against the enormous bruise on his forehead.

In the wheelhouse, Barrett gunned the trawler's engine to its maximum, his face ashen, a haunted, terrified look in his eyes.

Both men knew they had seen a ghost.

In time, the graveyard of warships became quiet once more, and the sanctuary of the great eel was once again undisturbed.

On the ocean's surface, ten miles from the battle-scarred fishing grounds, the beam of Scare-Point lighthouse flickered intermittently in the mists which held it in a vice-like grip.

THE FISH MARKET

Glass-eyed fish glare,
unwrapped on their pall of ice –
from what depths were you trawled,
cod, hake, lemon sole?

Sea-scent fuses with air,
eyes stare –
at young wives, old men,
and do you like them staring when,
ghosts haunt another place,
reverent of your living race?

And when in death we pay no heed,
for with sharp knives, we make you bleed,
then will your ghosts return to taunt,
ink-black waters that our trawlers haunt?

A BREED APART

Where the land ended and the sea began was often a mystery. Each of the great rivers which flowed into the bay had deposited centuries of sediment on the sandy, peaty shore. Vast areas of marshland had been created, which, without perception, had become one with the sea.

The marshes, still impenetrable in many places, and punctuated by tiny islands and pockets of forest, were the landscape of legends, and the inhabitants who dwelt therein, a people apart. Most kept to themselves, and outsiders – unless they became lost – remained on the periphery of this isolated environment.

On this day, one of the marshmen who still fished the flooded channels eased his punt through the swirling mists as dawn broke on an icy winter morning. In the reeds, a water rail called to its mate, and a bittern boomed in the distance. As the sky lightened and the mists vanished, the marshman moved closer to his traps. He moored his punt to an ancient wooden post which jutted out of the water on one side of the channel, then pulled his wicker baskets from the water.

The eels were small – no more than a foot long, not like the ones he had caught as a child when he had fished with Old Tom. Then, eels were fat, and often the length of a man's leg. These eels were small and skinny and would not sell well at market.

He emptied his meagre catch into a bucket at the bottom of his punt, then rebaited the baskets with shrimps before lowering them back into the flooded channel. As he moved along the channel, trap after trap came up the same, devoid of any eel of any size, and half were completely empty.

The children would go hungry once again.

The ramshackle cottage stood out like a beacon on the wooded islands amongst the mists. The peat walls and thatched roof had been home to marshmen for generations. The marshman warmed himself in front of an open fire, where cut turf and the occasional log burnt brightly in the hearth, preventing tentacles of ice from spreading insidiously into the cottage. With the children absent, away at their uncle's in a distant part of the marsh where the fishing was only marginally better, the marshman ate what little food he had. A couple of small eels, which he had smoked the previous year, and a small piece of stale bread made up his supper.

He wrapped himself in a thick woollen blanket, then drifted off to sleep in a rocking chair which had seen better days.

Beneath the full moon, the spirit of the marsh was taking shape. In the flooded channel, a will-o'-the-wisp began to take on human form. Glowing fire-red and holding a burning torch aloft, the figure, formed from the very gases in the marsh themselves, appeared to flicker, then hover above the reed beds, before moving inland as the great tide swept in.

That night, as the old marshman slipped into a long, deep sleep, warmed before a blazing hearth, his dreams of a full belly became a reality.

And the fairy-fire, the spirit of Old Tom? Well, it was not seen again for a generation. But the big eels were back, and they kept on coming. They sold well at market, and the children never went hungry again.

And the landscape, as ever, remained a place of legends.

And the people who dwelt therein remained, always, a breed apart.

OWL-NIGHT

I imagined them coupling
outside in the storm
in ivy-clad oak,
all beaks and claws
and a flurry of feathers.

And the dowry,
a fat rat.

And foraging for food,
ears pricked for the slightest sound,
bright eyes, mounted on chiselled cheekbones –
a pretty dormouse
shivers at the margins of mist.

In pellets,
the shattered bones
of shrews and mice.

THE SPECIMEN HUNTER

The specimen hunter arrived at the old fisherman's cottage just as the light was fading and the pipistrelle bats which roosted in the dusty attic began their nightly trawl for insects.

The cottage was redolent with age, and icons of fishing memorabilia, including stuffed pike and salmon weighing almost forty pounds, covered the walls. It was difficult to make out on the faded brass plaques the names of those anglers who'd caught the fish, but the young man guessed that some of the specimens, judging by their worn condition, must have been caught in the nineteenth century when Queen Victoria sat on the throne. He marvelled at the greenheart rods, horsehair lines, and enormous flies – the latter made from the feathers of rare and exotic birds – standing proud and erect in one corner of the room.

On the mantelpiece, above the hearth, he noticed the empty vase, so beautifully and intricately painted with an image of a man in top hat and tails hooking a salmon on a fast-flowing river. Then he remembered. Damn! He'd forgotten the flowers! The landlady had been adamant that he must purchase flowers to put in the vase, no doubt to perfume the room, which had an overpowering damp and musty smell that seemed to permeate the very walls themselves. But the young man's mind was on fish, and that specimen wild brown trout he intended to catch tomorrow. The flowers could wait; he'd pick some up later. Fishing, an obsession for the specimen hunter, could not.

He carried his bags to the bedroom, unpacked, took a quick shower, then, overcome by a creeping fatigue – he blamed it on the long drive from the city – slid seamlessly beneath the crisp sheets on the four-poster bed.

Outside, the night came alive. A tawny owl hooted from the treetop of an ancient oak, and roe deer foraged in the mists which lingered at the edge of the forest. The sounds of badgers snuffling and shuffling in the garden in their endless search for earthworms did nothing to disturb him. And even the cries of an old fox, barking from its secret haunt in the depths of the forest, did not interrupt his dreams of fish. The specimen hunter slept soundly throughout the night.

He rose early the next morning, cooked a light breakfast of two fried eggs and some toast, then made his way along an overgrown, twisting path in the direction of the river, which was hidden deep in a valley some half a mile from the cottage.

On the river, the young man cast a black gnat to the brown trout sunning themselves between the strands of water crowfoot. Through his polaroids he could see that there were some real specimens in this river, perhaps fish of over five pounds, but they were proving impossible to catch. He changed flies, moved stealthily from location to location, but with conditions against him as the summer sun beat down from a cloudless sky, he simply could not tempt a fish to take his fly. He left the river in the early evening, angry with himself that he did not catch anything. He would be back the next day to try again.

As he crossed the threshold of the cottage, the damp and musty smell, which had been overpowering on his arrival the previous day, now almost choked him. Briefly, he gagged, then remembered the flowers and the owner's strict instructions that he should buy some roses to place in the vase above the hearth. He attempted to chuckle. Perhaps there was method in her madness, after all! But he quickly dismissed those thoughts of flowers. He could put up with the smell and the damp; after all, he had fish to catch, and a specimen brown trout at that. He would have to rethink his tactics for the next day.

The cottage came alive at night. A full moon hung above the restless forest, which moved with the scuttling and rustlings of the creatures of the dark. An icy mist gripped the cottage as finger-like tendrils scratched, then permeated, the very stonework.

The young man slept, oblivious to the dank and odious presence which had entered his room. As that presence crept higher up the bed, it pressed and squeezed and suffocated. He barely moved as the last breath was stolen from his body. A bouquet of dead roses was placed next to his corpse.

The landlady, an old hag of indeterminate age, kept a collection in large glass cases in her cellar. The young man, strong and muscular as he was, would make a fine addition, and in the next few days, she would prepare then stuff him in a fly-fishing pose.

In the cellar, which appeared to have no entrance or exit, and which seemed to stretch to infinity, her collection was growing. There was a coracle fisherman from Wales, netting some sewin; and an Edwardian lord, smoking a pipe, complete with ghillie, hooking a mahseer from a raging torrent somewhere in India. And, of course, there was that very fine old Victorian gentleman, her first love, casting for salmon on a fast-flowing river in top hat and tails, a red rose gripped tightly between his polished teeth.

The old hag, a legendary water witch, cackled from somewhere deep in the darkest corner of the forest.

'They always forget the flowers!'

And, of course, she could never forgive them for that.

A TALE OF TWO RIVERBANKS

Close to where a line of verdant willows wept shade into the river, the old ferryman observed the otter cub leave the main watercourse then swim up the stream. When the cub dived, he watched bubbles rise to the surface, marking the otter's progress as it swam towards its holt.

As he stood on the riverbank, he pulled the woollen scarf tighter around his neck. Mists hung in the air, and the frigid air of an autumn morning brought a chill to the landscape.

In the distance, the sleek shape of the otter cub slid from the water, climbed up the riverbank, then disappeared into its holt, hidden beneath the tangled tree roots of a centuries-old oak.

Somewhere, not too distant from the jetty on which the ferryman now sat, the haunting cry of a roosting tawny owl permeated the silence.

The first customers for the ferry had yet to appear.

The old ferryman reached into his haversack and opened a flask of hot, steaming tea.

Despite the cold, he loved these misty mornings. They were so peaceful, and so uplifting.

And as he sipped on the sweet, black tea which slid down his throat like nectar, a kingfisher, bright as a blue spear, darted in front of him.

When he had finished his tea, he began to walk upstream, to place flowers on his wife's grave in the ancient chapel grounds.

He walked leisurely; despite his age, his legs were strong. The years of working his punt and an active rural lifestyle had maintained the strength in his wiry physique.

He listened to the sounds of the river as water tumbled over the weir in front of him. In the waterfall above the weir, a silver salmon leapt and twisted in the air. Air was not the salmon's natural element, but it appeared as if the fish was leaping for joy and was, for an instant, briefly at home in the chill autumn light.

As it flopped back into the river, to hide in a deep pool, it startled a pair of dippers, which flew out from where they had been nesting behind the curtain of spray. The old ferryman marvelled at these little birds; how they, too, could bestride both elements of air and water, just like the salmon. He loved to watch them and their white bibs as they bobbed up and down on their favourite rock before diving into the river to feed on the small creatures which lived under the stones near the water's edge.

As he climbed a twisting and winding path some distance above the river, the mists which had accompanied him in the valley simply vanished, and the ancient chapel loomed into view.

When he entered the churchyard, he stopped, then reached into his haversack, tenderly grasping the small bunch of flowers he had picked from his garden. Overcome by a sudden sadness, he shed a single tear as he knelt to place the pretty flowers against his wife's headstone. Slowly, he wiped that tear away with his handkerchief, then stood up.

He looked at the other graves, each meticulously tended, each adorned with fresh-cut blooms. In summer, he would spend more time in the churchyard, sitting on the grass and soaking up the sunshine, watching the garish butterflies flit along the hedgerow then settle upon the wildflowers which grew in untouched profusion amongst the headstones.

Reluctantly, he left the churchyard behind, then slowly headed back in the direction of the towpath, alongside the river.

Now, time passed quickly for the old ferryman, and lost in reverie as he was, early morning had merged into late afternoon before he knew it.

As he arrived back at the jetty, the autumn sun was already sinking below the horizon.

His first passengers were waiting, the mists swirling about them.

A pale, yellow moon hung in the darkening sky.

'Good evening, Mr Thomas.'

'Good evening, ma'am. How are your husband and the children?'

'Very well, Mr Thomas, very well!'

'Aah, and I see you have brought Shadow with you tonight. I assume he will be with you for the crossing?'

'Well, of course, Mr Thomas. What did you expect?'

The old ferryman did not reply, but a polite nod of acknowledgement and a warm smile of understanding passed fleetingly between them.

Climbing on board the punt, the family's complexions grew paler, mirroring that of the mists. Their dog, Shadow, a moth-eaten but wily old sheepdog was last to board.

The crossing was made in good, if quiet, humour, and the river remained calm.

As the punt touched the far riverbank and its adjoining jetty, the family of four prepared to disembark.

'I presume there will be no charge, tonight, Mr Thomas?'

'No, Mrs Jones. Is there ever?'

No one spoke again, and as the old ferryman watched the four figures disappear into the mists cloaking the ruined village, their wily old sheepdog close at heel, he pushed his punt into deeper water.

In a garden adjacent to one of the ruined cottages, Mrs Jones straightened up the tall, weather-beaten cross which was leaning to one side. She brushed the wet cobwebs from the crumbling old wood, then read aloud the inscription carved into its gnarled grain.

IN MEMORY OF ALL THOSE WHO DIED IN THE
GREAT FLOOD OF 1836.

Emily and James, the family's two young children, and their sheepdog, Shadow, had long since vanished into the woods to frolic in the trees.

Mr and Mrs Jones held hands as they walked amongst the ruins.

As the punt approached the far riverbank, a second family was waiting to make the crossing.

They, too, had pale complexions like the mists.

From somewhere in the darkness, came the haunting cry of a dog fox.

The sleek silhouette of an otter cub left its holt, then swam up the stream.

The night became peaceful, the river calm.

The old ferryman at one with the burgeoning silence.

RIVER DREAMS

Spun in a weed-strewn moon's reflection
are recollections,
where coracles swirled in salmon pools
on Tywi, Teifi, Taff –
of Dai the ferryman,
a rock for a pillow,
sound asleep.

Where otters creep,
willows weep shade into water canvas –
brush of feather-blue,
crush of lovers' limbs,
cool summer pools.

In the dew,
spirits' feet,
where two tides meet,
and 'Croeso I Gymru,'
becomes 'Welcome to Wales.'

LADY OF THE LAKE

The lake shimmered in the oppressive heat. Clouds of midges swarmed in their millions, rising like a dark, billowing blanket to the top of the shattered scree slope.

The swallows had swept in moons ago, crossing the vast sands of the Sahara Desert, flying over the sea, and skirting the Atlas Mountains of Morocco, before arriving at their summer feeding grounds. Their pilgrimage north now saw them nesting in the abandoned farmhouses and barns dotted about the edge of the lake. And now, as they darted amongst the clouds of midges, snapping up insects with their tiny beaks, they gorged themselves, for soon, like the midges, they would be gone.

In the cold, clear waters of the brook, the lady of the stream – a grayling of indeterminate age, and over three pounds in weight, drifted nonchalantly in the rich, oxygenated water. Fish-fry flashed about her, flickering silver and gold amongst the water crowfoot and across the sun-drenched gravel.

The grayling was carried by the current into the lake. As she rose to take a fly on the surface, she extended her large dorsal fin, and her mouth sucked in the tiny morsel.

Languidly, she swam deeper, and the underwater landscape loomed large before her. A sunken rowing boat appeared in the distance, part-obscured by tall, dense banks of weeds, which rose from the lakebed, seeking the warm rays of the summer sun. Above her, lily pads cast dark shadows in the shallows, whilst shoals of bleak, roach, and rudd meandered about the submerged forest, safe from the jaws of predatory pike.

The grayling swam deeper, and more familiar objects loomed into view.

She swam towards the shelf, as she always had. She had known the reef on the shelf for many years. It had provided her with shelter and sanctuary when she was young, and now, it drew her like a magnet.

Sunlight glinted on the lake's surface, and her silver flanks flashed as she rolled.

The thing, bound with ropes and wrapped in a carpet, swayed in the current.

From beneath the carpet, a large eel emerged, momentarily becoming entangled in the hair of the thing, before returning to its lair. Lead piping, encased in concrete, anchored the thing to the reef.

When divers found the body of Suzie Jones, she had been in the lake for over twenty years.

She was identified by dental records.

Months later, her husband was arrested, tried, and found guilty of her murder. He survives to this very day.

Soon afterwards, anchored to the reef, where the body of Suzie Jones had been entombed for so many years, a small, marble cross was erected in her memory.

As the lady of the stream swam towards the shelf, the new thing loomed into view. Nonchalantly, she swam amongst the strands of weed, tangled like human hair, which clung to the marble.

The swallows would return soon, and once again the lake would shimmer in the oppressive heat, and clouds of midges would swarm once more, rising like a dark, billowing blanket to the top of the shattered scree.

PIT PONIES

The old miner fished the flooded quarry on occasion. His mind was not what it used to be, but fishing relaxed him and brought back memories of his youth, of when he was strong, fit, and vigorous. He fished with light tackle, from an old wooden platform jutting out from the weed-covered bank for the flotillas of red-finned roach and rudd which patrolled the shallows of the cold, clear waters.

The quarry held many secrets. Huge pike the size of crocodiles and great eels like miniature anacondas were rumoured to inhabit its dark and tangled depths. On the spartan cliffs which towered above its steeply wooded sides, ravens and peregrine falcons had constructed their stick-like nests. And amongst the reeds, in the hidden recesses of the mist-shrouded margins, the ghostly boom of a single bittern would often echo for miles across the secluded body of water.

The old miner felt a sharp tug on his line and watched the tip of his vintage cane rod bow to the water's surface. He reeled in a beautiful, scale-perfect roach of about one pound, then quickly unhooked and released it, only to watch it vanish back into the depths from whence it came.

A pair of courting swans, their plumage as white as snow, drifted spectrally in and out of the mist which was now swirling across the pool. He felt a second sharp tug on his line and unhurriedly reeled in a tiny rudd, which weighed no more than a few ounces. He lovingly cradled the fish in one hand, admiring its unbridled beauty, before, once again, releasing it back into the icy depths. From somewhere in the woods high above him, the unearthly 'Kee-wik! Kee-wik!' of a tawny owl brought him back to reality with a shudder.

It had been more than fifty years since the accident in the mine, but the memories of the tragedy were still both vivid and painful for the old man. His thoughts meandered back to the days of his youth, and how he'd cared for and managed his beloved pit ponies. In the shaft mine the ponies had been stabled underground; it was his responsibility to muck out and feed them on a diet of chopped hay and maize, and bring them to the surface for respite from their arduous and dangerous work beneath the earth. Typically, the ponies would work an eight-hour day, during which they could easily haul thirty tons of coal in coal tubs along the narrow-gauge railway. An average lifespan for a pony was no more than four years, so anything the old miner could do to prolong and improve the quality of his horses' lives made him feel content.

A particular favourite of his had been the white stallion called Pegasus, the strongest and most sure-footed pony he had ever known. Pegasus had lived a long life hauling those heavy coal tubs in the bowels of the earth, but then the old miner had taken particular care of him and had given him extra rations when he could. And Pegasus could eat! Oh, how that stallion could eat!

But those times were long gone, and Pegasus and all the other pit ponies had gone with them. And now, as dusk approached, the old miner was alone with his memories and his vintage cane rod.

His rod bowed once more to the water's surface, and once again he was cradling a beautiful, scale-perfect rudd of perhaps half a pound in the palm of his hand. He slipped it back into the pool, and it swam off into the ethereal depths.

Other creatures were about now; a dog fox barked from somewhere in the distance, and tiny bats swept the pool's surface for any small insects they could find. A sharp wind picked up, masking the tunnelling and scuttling of the smaller creatures in the undergrowth.

The wind also masked the first footfalls of the larger animals. But he knew they'd come. They always did, once a year, on the anniversary of the explosion which had destroyed and flooded the mine. He could hear them now, their hooves clip-clopping on the woodland paths which wound down through the trees.

The old miner put down his rod, put his hand into his pocket, and reached for the large, cubed sugar lumps he knew they liked. Through the mists he moved gradually towards them. It was the white stallion which nuzzled his chest first, then one pony after another did the same. He greeted them like long-lost friends; he stroked them, offering each one a sugar lump and running his wiry fingers through their damp manes and along their powerful backs. He felt their cold breath on his face and sensed the longing, knowing look in their dark eyes.

Time seemed to have no meaning now, and as the sky blackened and a full moon emerged from behind its shield of freezing cloud, the old miner watched the pit ponies vanish like spectres into the trees. He followed, melting into the ether.

As the sun rose above the haunted pool, little moved, except the mists and the swan spirits which swirled across the water's surface, and the shoals of red-finned roach and rudd which patrolled the margins of its icy depths.

THE HAUNTED GARDEN

Hidden in the old tree stump where the cat scratched and sniffed, below where the ivy crept along the wall and behind the tangle of holly and brambles, the dormouse slept.

The old house, now just a ruin, was almost concealed by the mists which had risen from the cool waters of the lake, mists which now billowed into every crack and crevice of the crumbling structure.

In the deepest parts of the lake, beside the great dam, the descendants of the wild carp introduced to the tranquil waters by the monks centuries before had grown huge in their pristine isolation.

As the spring sun rose above the horizon and warmed the surface of the water, the mists faded, and the first dragonflies and damselflies took to the wing.

In the walled garden, a stoat, still partly clothed in its winter coat, moved sinuously amongst the broken stones at the base of the wall. Her kits, well hidden behind a pile of old logs and moss, huddled together for warmth whilst their mother hunted for rats and rabbits in the undergrowth. Songbirds bathed in the lichen-encrusted fountains; fountains which had long ceased functioning, but whose weathered cherubs still held up their arms in supplication, as if seeking salvation from the skies above. The trees swayed in the light breeze, and as the sun rose higher in those clear, azure-blue skies, butterflies with orange-tipped wings swept the corridors of the secret maze.

The garden was at peace, and still the dormouse slept.

By late afternoon, the wild carp, as if drawn by some invisible, inexorable force, left the seclusion of their weed-strewn isolation and swam up the water column. As dusk inched ever closer to darkness, the mists rose once again from the water's surface, enveloping the old house in a white, billowing shawl. A lone hooded figure drifted in and out of those mists as they swirled at the edge of the lake. He moved, as he had done so for generations now, almost imperceptibly to an anointed spot at the top of the great dam. As night descended like a black curtain, the first of the great fishes' mouths broke the water's surface. In the hypnotic moonlight, their huge, ghost-white shapes lit up the surface of the lake like creatures from ancient mythology. The hooded figure, so pale beneath his habit, broke and tossed leavened bread to them as he had done now for so many years.

In the distance, badgers emerged from their sett, and a long-eared owl swept silently through the trees.

Along the wall where the ivy crept, a ragged old tomcat of some great, yet indeterminable age dropped to his familiar scratching post in the tangle of holly and brambles at the base of the old tree stump.

From somewhere deep in the mists sounded a peal of chapel bells.

The lake, tranquil as ever, slipped seamlessly into the magic of dreamtime.

The garden was at peace, with its secrets.

And still the dormouse slept.

PEREGRINES ON THE CLOCK TOWER

(CARDIFF CITY HALL)

THE TIERCEL

Perched on a stone cherub,
above a boneyard of birds,
with his brutal beak, hangman's hood –
he was hardly angelic,
only the white eyelid flickering,
that moist, nictitating membrane,
briefly obscuring the black eye.

Then, hooked on the sky,
arcing for the stoop,
with fierce, ebony talons,
and eerie, piercing cry.

'KEK-KEK! KEK-KEK!'

THE FALCON

Yet, watching a chick through a scope,
a female falcon,
flapping, and hopping on bone-ledge,
playing with the carcass of a pigeon,
as a kitten, or puppy, would play with a toy –
was almost comical.

Yet, soon, she too would stoop from the sun,
with an adult's precision,
a perfect, peregrine incision –
slicing the sky.

*N.B. A tiercel is the name given to a male peregrine fal-
con. Tiercel is French for 'third'.*

*The male peregrine is a third smaller than a female, which
is called a falcon.*

SHE STOOPS TO CONQUER

The peregrine flew high over the city. Far below, myriad gulls soared and wheeled upon the thermals which shimmered in the heat of the summer skies. Born some distance to the south, two years before, on the storm-lashed cliffs of Southerndown, she had flown inland to seek a mate and raise a brood of young on a ledge of the clock tower of City Hall.

Her vision was acute; so acute in fact that she could see a student reading a book from a mile away. She paid little heed to the girl, who was lounging lazily on the lawns in front of the civic buildings, but instead focused the dark pupils of her eyes on the pigeons resting amongst the stonework. Her mate, known as a tiercel, sat motionless on one of the stone cherubs which jutted out from a ledge just below the clock face. Two of their young, a male and a female, hunkered down in the nest to avoid the torment of biting flies and summer heat. A third chick, another female, and the strongest of the three, used her claws and head to nudge the carcass of a woodcock along the ledge on which their nest of sticks was located. With her sharp beak, she picked at the scant remains of the carcass.

A few hundred feet below, powerful telescopes and binoculars were being trained on the nest from an RSPB marquee staked out on the lush grass. Searching questions were being asked of one of their volunteers.

'Do they eat mice, and can I have one as a pet?' screeched an excited young girl of about ten years of age.

The volunteer laughed out loud, then explained that occasionally peregrines would take mice, but their main prey was pigeons, and that it was not appropriate to have one as a pet.

At first, the girl seemed disappointed, but she soon perked up as the volunteer explained how the peregrines had come to nest in the city, then how they had chased some ravens from the clock tower before commandeering the ravens' nest of sticks.

He continued to entrance the excitable school party with further gems about the birds, including the fact that the peregrine was the fastest bird in the world and could fly at speeds up to 200 miles per hour in a stoop as it dispatched its prey.

All the children were eager to use the telescopes and binoculars to view the birds.

As the school party moved on into the museum, the volunteer sensed a newfound fascination amongst the children for the birds of prey. He hoped that fascination would last for the rest of their lives.

Far above all the commotion on the ground, the adult female peregrine began her arcing flight towards the heavens. As she gained height, moving effortlessly into the azure blue, the bronze hands of the clock struck midday. In the brilliant sunlight, some two miles above the marquee below, she folded back her slate-grey wings, tucked in her legs, and began to stoop. The pigeon knew nothing as it was struck at 200 miles per hour with a clenched foot like a steel mace, which broke its neck in an instant.

As the falcon swooped beneath her prey to grasp the dead bird in her claws, a single drop of bright red blood plummeted to earth, smearing the pages of a book which lay open in front of a student who lounged lazily on the lawns in front of the civic buildings. It was entitled *She Stoops to Conquer*, a play by the Irish writer, Oliver Goldsmith.

It was the student's shrieks of alarm which startled the crowds, and not the screeching of the falcon, which carried the dead bird to the nest to be plucked.

The shrill, eerie cries of her chicks cut through the oppressive summer heat.

Systematically, the falcon's beak worked like a scalpel as she opened the flesh.

A SEASONED OLD MOTH

The hawkmoth crawled up the window; his feathery antennae flickering against the glass.

He was only small, insignificant to some, yet his desire for escape was overwhelming. He had been trapped this way before; drawn through a gap in the window by the golden glow of the house lights.

Lights fascinated him and lured him like a magnet. And although there was danger in some, these particular beacons in the blackness had never threatened him.

As he crawled higher, he felt the cool draft of perfumed air which meant freedom.

When he beat his wings, blood flowed into their web-like veins, and he leapt from the window ledge.

The hawkmoth flew over the pines, skimming the treetops. Here he felt safe from the fierce creatures which hunted the darkness. A bat had almost speared him with its razor-sharp teeth, but he had managed to escape, emitting piercing, squeaking sounds from his throat to confuse the bat's sonar.

He had dived for the sanctuary of the great forest, to hide amongst the lichens and mosses of an ancient oak.

He was lucky; his entire body and both of his wings remained intact. In a matter of hours, he had made a full recovery.

Other creatures threatened the hawkmoth too. At night, cats, spiders' webs, and flashing headlights had claimed many of his kin.

He rarely flew by day; it was too dangerous. Despite the large, eye-like markings on his hindwings which, when exposed, could frighten predators, he chose to rest amongst the trees until the sun went down.

The hawkmoth sensed the presence of the yellow moon and white, pinpoint stars in the heavens.

Surprisingly, these too had once been a threat. For he had tried to fly to them on one occasion, spiralling into the endless black night like some winged angel, until, overcome by exhaustion, he had plummeted back to earth.

It was the great pine forest which had saved him once more, breaking that never-ending fall with its spongy canopy of leaves.

Then there was the time that he had flown too close to the orange flames of a bonfire. Many of his kin before him, hypnotised by such a warm glow, had not escaped so lightly and had been cremated instantly as they fell into the flames.

But then this hawkmoth was a seasoned old moth. He had learnt much about danger, and although now ravenous with hunger, he sensed the first rays of the morning sun.

He would feed tomorrow. Tonight, he would seek out the sanctuary of a great green pine.

The following evening, the hawkmoth again found himself drawn through a gap in the window. He had fed on the sweet nectar of a forest rose, which had invigorated him and enabled him to fly far.

Strange scents came to him as he struggled for a grip on the glass.

Here, it was warm. Not like the raging heat of a bonfire, but a comforting, seductive warmth.

It was the yellow light which had first attracted him; its golden glow in the blackness which had drawn him through the open shop window.

To his right, a new light flickered, and with the intoxicating nectar flowing through his veins, his judgement became clouded.

As he flew towards that light, its electric blueness baffled, then fried his tiny brain.

'Glad you bought that flycatcher, eh, Terry?'

'Yea, I hate damn moths! They get everywhere!' the shop owner growled. He grunted as he wiped his nose on his shirtsleeve before serving up more greasy chips.

By morning, the flycatcher was ready for emptying, and the hawkmoth, just one more insect glued to its grill.

Some days later, not far away, in a water meadow close to the great pine forest, the first small caterpillars were emerging from their eggs. As sunlight glistened in the dewdrops of the morning, and the busying of buzzing insects filled the air, the female hawkmoth nestled against a tree trunk to rest.

THE RIVER BECKONS
FOR A LAST CAST

I wink at you through splinters of starlight,
weeds trail like green limbs,
and as coracles swirl in your subconscious,
I know I'll pull you in.

So, bury me in a creel made of wicker,
and make this my last cast,
drop me in a favourite river,
but do not stand on the bank and weep.

Think of the time we cast a line
on Twyi, Teifi, Taff,
and dream in the reeds where the bittern cries,
where swallows sweep flies from the shallows.

And where the river narrows,
where the big trout lie,
think fondly of old Dai –

of recollections,
swan-white reflections,
and foxgloves fingered by bees.

And when the wind breathes,
before storm clouds intercede,
maybe, just maybe, I'll sense your soft-shoe shuffle.

So, bury me in a creel made of wicker,
and make this my last cast,
but do not stand on the bank and weep,
I am not dead, but in your sleep.

Author Profile

Marc Harris was born in Cardiff, Wales, in 1962.

Marc has previously written four books. *South and West Wales: Its Wildlife, People and Places,* a book devoted to the natural world in that part of the United Kingdom, was published in 2022. His other books include *Wild Tales & Rural Rides,* a book of short stories, travel, and nature writing. He has also published poems in a poetry pamphlet *Sentience: 14 Poems,* and a further book of poetry, *Rhythms of Nature.*

Marc has also written articles and short stories for many magazines, *including Evergreen, The Countryman, This England* and *Explore England.* He has always been a lover of horror, gothic tales and ghost stories.

He now divides his time between a house in the Vale of Glamorgan and a caravan with stunning views of the sea overlooking the Bristol Channel. He lives with his two rescue cats, which keep him company and entertained, and which he adores.

What Did You Think of
Wild and Uncanny Tales?

A big thank you for purchasing this book. It means a lot that you chose this book specifically from such a wide range on offer. I do hope you enjoyed it.

Book reviews are incredibly important for an author. All feedback helps them improve their writing for future projects and for developing this edition. If you are able to spare a few minutes to post a review on Amazon, that would be much appreciated.

Publisher Information

Rowanvale Books provides publishing services to independent authors, writers and poets all over the globe. We deliver a personal, honest and efficient service that allows authors to see their work published, while remaining in control of the process and retaining their creativity. By making publishing services available to authors in a cost-effective and ethical way, we at Rowanvale Books hope to ensure that the local, national and international community benefits from a steady stream of good quality literature.

For more information about us, our authors or our publications, please get in touch.

www.rowanvalebooks.com
info@rowanvalebooks.com

Printed in the USA
CPSIA information can be obtained
at www.ICGtesting.com
LVHW021759140923
758110LV00005B/455